D1412379

What Difference Does It Make, Danny?

By the same author

Magic Balloon, Sleeping Chair
A Throne For Sesame
Wide-Awake Jake

What Difference
Does It Make, Danny?

Helen Young

Pictures by Quentin Blake

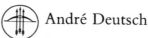 André Deutsch

First published 1980 by
André Deutsch Limited
105 Great Russell Street London WC1

Set, printed and bound in Great Britain by
Fakenham Press Limited, Fakenham, Norfolk

British Library Cataloguing in Publication Data

Young, Helen, *b.1938*
    What difference does it make, Danny?
    I. Title
    823'.9'1J   PZ7.Y864

    ISBN 0-233-97248-X

First published in the United States of America 1980

Library of Congress Number 80-65665

1

That year, the most eventful of Danny Blane's life, the school went to the country for Sports Day. At least, it seemed like the country to the bus-loads of children. Their destination was a large estate about twenty-five miles from their school.

After heats run on concrete playgrounds, the grass of a vast parkland was like cushioned velvet to their feet. Alongside the mown tracks, which teachers had cordoned off the day before with stakes and tapes, the grass grew high and wild. And beyond the children could see a river.

They stood in uncertain little groups when they left the coaches until suddenly a sense of freedom spread amongst them, like an outbreak of spring fever. Some turned cartwheels; some tried to. Games of chase sprang up and led nowhere as children leaped joyfully in the air or on top of each other, or simply flung themselves on the bouncy, welcoming grass.

The head teacher let them enjoy it for as long as possible before calling everyone to order. Good-natured staff, seeming somehow younger and more human in this setting, herded children into lines and

Miss North, the headmistress, smiled sympathetically. The sun was high and a clean green smell wafted round them. She could imagine how difficult it was to stand in disciplined queues listening to a lecture, but she wanted to remind them they were still under school rules.

They had heard it all before, of course.

The gravest sin was litter-dropping and wild flowers were not for picking. Tracy Smith who had gathered a wispy bunch of buttercups and yarrow, blushed hot and tried to hide her bouquet behind her skinny back. With presence of mind, her friend Eliza snatched it and presented it with great charm, to Miss North.

With an exaggerated shocked look followed by a warning frown and finally a smile at such daring, Miss North accepted the offering and the children laughed. Parents who had come to help were spreading cloths on the ground a little distance away for the marvellous picnic which would follow the races. They looked up, at the laughter, to see what the joke was.

Miss North was merciful and kept her talk short. She reminded them it was a privilege to be invited, what was considered good behaviour and what most certainly was not.

Feet shifted in the lines and children adopted a virtuous look, to speed the end of the sermon.

'And keep away from the river,' she ended up. 'Until it's time for the picnic.'

Frantic whispering broke out in Miss Pringle's group of eight and nine-year-olds. These were Pringle's Pets, the class Miss North regarded as 'spirited', known occasionally to the rest of the staff as 'Pringle's Pests'. Miss Pringle, who taught that age group from choice and always regarded her class as the best in the school, usually referred to them as 'my little horrors'.

'You ask, Danny,' hissed a boy named Billy Caster, who had reasons of his own connected with regular uncomfortable visits to Miss North's office, for not wanting to draw attention to himself.

Danny didn't mind. He thrust up a hand.

'Miss ... can we swim, miss?' asked Danny and a traditional chorus of encouragement swelled from all the ranks.... 'Miss, miss, miss.'

'We've brought our swimming things, miss,' called Danny, the soloist. 'Sir said.'

'I've forgotten mine,' one small child wailed, echoed by several others.

'Good. One or two less to keep an eye on,' muttered an unsympathetic teacher not sure it was a good idea to let a whole school loose in a river, however shallow and slow moving.

'Can we, miss?' persisted Danny.

'Some of you *can*,' said Miss North who was very keen on the difference between 'can' and 'may' and never forgot she was a teacher, even standing in the middle of a field. 'Whether or not you *may* depends on how well you all behave during the Sports.'

Well skilled at interpreting Miss North, the children took this to mean almost certainly yes, and looked at each other hopefully.

Miss North smiled indulgently and dismissed them to run to their groups for the start of the races.

Danny had discussed his chances before leaving home that morning.

'Will you bring home a medal?' his father asked.

'Not unless Wayne runs backwards and Billy stays at home,' he answered cheerfully. He was not a pessimist but he was realistic.

And for once they could all believe what they were told each year; that it did not matter if they won or lost. Taking part was pure pleasure in such a place. Danny remembered the hot, hard thudding of the heats and felt he could run barefoot along these welcoming tracks. Better times were clocked up for those races than ever recorded in the history of the school.

The games master noted the times in a leather-bound book and felt a slightly sad pride. He was to retire at the end of the term and these were his last sports.

'Look at them,' he said to a new teacher who was helping him time the events. 'Winged ruddy colts, aren't they? If they'd run like that on the football pitch, I'd have the junior league cup on my mantelpiece. Some of those lads would do anything to get out of football. "Sir, I've lost a boot." "Sir, I've forgotten my strip." That Danny Blane even had a fit once, rather than play.'

The new teacher looked a little startled and the games master laughed. 'Well that's what I said to him afterwards, anyway. Just my little joke. Danny didn't mind.'

'You mean, he really had a fit?' The new teacher still looked as though he thought it a joke in poor taste.

'Oh yes. He's quite liable to do that, is Danny. Not deliberately, of course. And he hasn't had one since, come to think of it. It's well under control in his case.'

'You mean he's an epileptic?' said the teacher, surprised.

'You'd better not let Danny hear you say that. He'll tell you that's old fashioned. He has epilepsy, he'll tell you. Not that it bothers him much, I must say.'

The new teacher looked at Danny in fascination.

'He doesn't look like an epileptic, does he?' he said.

The games master looked a little impatient. 'What do you expect?' he asked. 'Horns? He doesn't look like a little devil either, but he can be. And he's not going to win this race by the looks of it.'

Wayne Dunstan had streaked past Danny to win the 100 yards. Billy triumphed in the obstacle race. Just when Danny thought he had the spoon and potato sewn up, Wayne with the comical rolling gait he'd copied from long distance walkers, rollicked past him.

In the end, Danny had three second prizes to collect and the lady who had come to present them had begun to smile when his name was called.

'You're a good loser,' she commented, when he came up beaming for the third time. The children had no curiosity about her identity, but she was the owner of the land and liked to invite city children to enjoy it.

Danny shrugged. 'I'm not the best at running,' he said philosophically.

'What are you best at?' the lady asked. 'Or are you too modest to say?'

'Swimming,' Danny replied promptly.

She seemed quite pleased to hear that. 'You do swimming, do you,' she said approvingly. 'Good. Then I'll let you into a secret.' She leant towards him and said something very quietly.

'What did she say?' demanded his friends when Danny returned.

He smirked. 'She asked what was an intelligent, good-looking lad like me doing with a bunch of punks like you,' he said and yelled when Wayne whacked him with his first prize, a book about athletics.

'She said I'd find that book helpful,' remarked Wayne.

The picnic was great. The mothers had held meetings to decide what to bring and they had all made a special effort for the food was to be communal. The sandwiches were called heroes – french bread sliced longways twice and piled with mixtures like ham, cheese, egg, tomato, salami and all with lettuce and mayonnaise. Mouths had to open very wide to accommodate a hero sandwich and no one who ate one could afford the luxury of dignity. For the more sedate there were cold chicken legs and sausage rolls, hard-boiled eggs and salads in little plastic containers. The salads were popular with the teachers.

'Don't like salad. Never have,' remarked one little girl complacently, her fist crammed with a hero packed

with more salad per bite than she had ever experienced in her life. Her mother was about to point this out when common-sense came over her and she grinned instead. 'That's right, love,' she advised. 'Stick to what you fancy.'

The teachers' contribution was ice-cream in insulated containers. The children were worried in case there wouldn't be enough to go round. But there was.

Afterwards they played, a bit more lazily now, in the long overgrown parts of the park, while adults slumped blissfully under trees and mothers chatted idly to each other about how nice it would be to move out of the city and live somewhere like this.

Danny lay on his stomach, chewing a long stem of grass, and wondered if the lady had forgotten the secret she told him.

At two o'clock they were told they could put on swimming gear which they did with varying degrees of modesty. There was giggling, much hiding behind tree trunks and a lot of showing off. When they had changed, Miss North called them together for another announcement and Danny knew this was it.

'We have a surprise event,' said Miss North, looking around with a pleased expression on her face. 'And . . .' she paused for dramatic effect. 'It's to be an annual event. That's right. You have all behaved so well we've been invited to come again.'

To her this was clearly the important part of the announcement. Other schools, she said darkly, had not been invited back after their first visit. Naturally the headmistress went on a bit about that, and how she was proud of them, while parents looked fondly at their children. Danny was more interested in the details of the special event and finally Miss North got round to it.

There was, she told them, a natural pool farther up the river. Good swimmers (and good swimmers only) were invited to compete in races and there would be a cup which the overall winner would keep for a year.

That was the secret he had been told. Danny hoped the lady did not expect him to win, but he was very pleased to be good enough to take part. Would-be entrants were weeded out by the games master who knew exactly what stage they had all reached. Wayne, who had failed his bronze, was furious and Billy Caster couldn't even swim.

'Sir, I can do a length in the public baths,' protested Wayne.

'With water wings? Next please.'

Danny was one of the first to reach the pool and the sight of it made him gasp because it was so beautiful. The public baths were going to seem a bit tame after this.

The only way in was to dive.

Someone had created a home-made board, which was really just a plank, and while some lined up on that, others launched themselves from the rocky sides in joyful chaos.

It was clear and deep and felt wetter, colder, fresher than any water they had ever been in. The games

master had to blow himself puce on his whistle before
the pool was cleared so that races could be organised.
Danny swam underwater to the edge then hauled himself out, shaking the hair which had plastered itself to
his face and waiting, as he blinked, for the eye-
smarting which always followed a swim. It did not
happen and it took him a few moments to work out
why. No chlorine.

17

The games master was at his happiest organising heats and in a pool this size they were over quickly. He pitted girls against girls; boys against boys; then matched the winners by age. The possible permutations baffled most of the other teachers, but he revelled in complications. It had been said of him that he enjoyed working out the football timetables a great deal more than the actual games and his ability was at full stretch now.

He had brought the competitors to a final before his assistant had finished working out who should swim against whom, and to Danny's great pleasure, he had a place in it. It suddenly dawned on him he might even win. The best swimmer he was up against was a wiry girl named Kathy, and, in great honesty, Danny knew he would not normally beat her. But Kathy had run more races that day than Danny and he had noticed she was tiring. He told himself not to count on it – but he thought he could do it.

And he did. The screams of his classmates, echoed by the staff, for everyone liked Danny, drowned the umpire's whistle and could be heard as far as the lazy few who had stayed by the picnic ground.

His mother, noted for her calm in a crisis but who went to pieces in moments of joy, dabbed her eyes with a handkerchief, and the first, when she had got her breath, to congratulate him was Kathy.

'You're a good winner, too,' smiled the lady who owned the park. Danny was shivering now with a towel round him and she handed him a silver cup which she promised to have engraved later.

'And a good advertisement,' she added.

'For the school?' asked Danny uneasily. He never cared for that line of chat.

'For epilepsy,' said the lady, surprising him. 'I'm very interested in epilepsy. That's why Miss North mentioned you to me. One of my own children has it and I quite often give talks on the subject. I shall tell a lot of people about you – if you don't mind.'

Danny didn't mind. He was longing to get away to show the cup to his friends. He'd had epilepsy for so long he hardly ever thought about it, but this was the first cup he had ever won.

2

Danny was two when he first had a convulsion. He was often asked by friends who had never got so far as an out-patients what it had been like. Was it true he'd been taken in an ambulance with its siren on and how long had he had to stay in hospital.

It was certainly true about the ambulance but, to his regret, Danny did not remember much about the trips he made then. He did remember his hospital visits because he enjoyed them so much.

He was first taken to casualty because his parents had no idea what was wrong with him. He had been in bed asleep when they heard him cry out. They rushed to his bedroom and found him shuddering as if a giant hand was shaking him.

Danny's mother could be forgiven for doing all the wrong things, because she'd never seen a major fit before and it can be quite alarming to someone who doesn't know how to cope. So she picked him up and hugged him while his father rang for an ambulance and by the time Danny had recovered he was in hospital.

He had to make quite a few trips after that because occasionally instead of having just one convulsion,

Danny had several and when that happened he had to be given an injection to stop the attacks.

His doctor suggested a spell in hospital so that tests could be done to find out why he was more liable than most people to have fits. Danny's mother began to prepare him for his stay away from home. She bought a book about children in hospital and read it to him every night, but she needn't have bothered. Danny liked what he had seen about hospitals. He couldn't wait to go.

He liked what they had to eat in hospital – sausage, chips and ice-cream. And he knew the nurses would give him tea which he never had at home. His previous visits had seemed all too short to Danny.

His mother, following the staff nurse, led him to the ward and Danny was shown his bed. It had pull-up sides like a cot and Danny, who had been in a proper bed at home for months, did not think too highly of that. He was quite happy to climb on it until he noticed that the other cots in the room all had children already in them. In the middle of the day! Danny jumped quickly down in case he was trapped, and went to look at the other children. He felt sorry for them because he could see they were not really well enough to enjoy being in hospital.

'He can have his nap now,' suggested the nurse, hopefully.

'I'm afraid he's given up sleeping in the day,' said Danny's mother. She sounded apologetic and the nurse certainly looked as though this was bad news. Danny was doing his best to cheer up one little girl by rattling

the bars of her cot and jumping up and down making his chimpanzee face. She appreciated that but the duty nurse didn't and Danny was taken firmly to the vast toy-strewn playroom.

'Here's Danny come to play with you,' said the nurse brightly to the three or four other children in the room, as though he had been brought to hospital purely for their entertainment. They looked at him without interest and returned to their puzzles and bricks. A boy a little bigger than Danny pushed him then stood back to see what would happen. Danny, delighted to have found a friend, pushed him back.

They became known as the terrible twins, those
two, and they had a marvellous time. The nurses
didn't. They were used to quiet, sick children. Danny
and his new friend were much too lively.

For the first day they were content to ride the pedal
car and the tricycle in the playroom, but by the next

day they had burst out into the corridors. They zoomed up and down, scaring the life out of the sister and dive-bombing the doctors.

The other boy was in for tests too, for some quite different condition and the nurses began to welcome the times when one or other was taken off to see a doctor.

Danny, too, enjoyed these interludes. He had been quick to spot that there was always a bowl of sweets on the desk and rightly guessed these were for those who behaved well. Danny behaved very well.

The only test he found rather boring was the e.e.g., short for electro-encephalogram, a machine which can measure brain waves. If Danny had been older he might have found that idea fascinating, but at two and a half he quickly lost interest in what was a long, tedious business. He had small discs attached to various parts of his head with glue and was told they were called electrodes. These were in turn attached by wires to the e.e.g. recording machine which scribbled inky graphs over reams of paper while Danny looked at picture books, closed his eyes, watched flashing lights and became so tired of the whole process he almost went to sleep. The e.e.g. did not hurt, but removing the glue from his hair afterwards wasn't much fun.

There were blood tests too.

More than one doctor wanted a blood sample from Danny and he became quite conceited about his own bravery. He was in fact quite a courageous little boy, but the truth was that, apart from a slight jab when the needle went in, these tests did not hurt much.

Everyone seemed to expect him to make a fuss, and when he didn't, there was a lot of praise. Praise on these occasions equalled extra sweets, and Danny was in favour of that.

His friend had made such a fuss about his blood test that Danny heard the screams from two doors away.

'*I* didn't cry,' said Danny.

'I did,' said the other boy simply and seemed to think this just as much an occasion for pride.

Danny did quite a lot of exploring in hospital and found it all very interesting. He visited a casualty ward and saw children in plaster, one with more bandages than the invisible man and quite a number with drips beside their beds. There was quite a fuss about that because his own nurses realised he was missing. They looked under beds and into cupboards for a bit, calling his name, and one of them ran distractedly down to the main hall to ask if anyone had seen him leave the hospital.

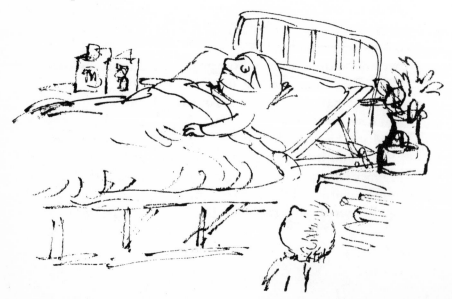

That excitement came to an end when the casualty sister took a second look at Danny, realised he was not one of hers, read his wrist band and returned him to his own ward. He was pounced on by three relieved nurses who hugged and scolded him in turns which left Danny unmoved because he could not think why they were making a fuss. After that he had a label pinned to his jersey which read: 'Property of Eliza Ward. If found, please return.'

When he was asked later what he liked best about hospital, he said 'the lift'. It was his greatest pleasure and he found it simple to slide in behind a group of adults. He would ride happily up and down until someone noticed and read his label and returned him to his ward. His great hope was to find himself alone in the lift so he could work it himself, but that never happened and it was just as well because Danny could never have reached the control buttons.

It seemed to Danny that almost every part of him had been tested for something, even his head had been measured, and finally the results were given to his parents.

There was nothing wrong with Danny at all.

He had epilepsy all right and would be given medicine to stop him having fits, but no one could tell why. His parents were both relieved and dismayed. It was good to know nothing nasty was causing the fits. But epilepsy! Just the sound of the word worried them. They both had vague, frightening notions about it and they asked a lot of worried questions.

Would it affect his behaviour? His intelligence? Would Danny have to go to a special school?

'No, no and no,' said the consultant and Danny's parents were lucky to have this particular man dealing with Danny. He knew a great deal about epilepsy and he also knew a lot about people's reactions to it. He was aware how many strange ideas there are about this condition and he answered questions they hadn't even liked to ask.

He advised them to read all they could about epilepsy. 'It's a fascinating subject,' he said. 'There are more myths and superstitions surrounding epilepsy than any other condition I can think of. Just remember, it's not a disease. There's nothing shameful about it. It can happen to anyone. Just give Danny his medicine regularly and he'll have very few attacks.'

And when he saw them out, he added: 'And treat him like an ordinary chap, for that's what he is. Except he's a bit more of a character than most. We're going to miss him around here.'

Danny's parents watched him anxiously for a week or two, convinced he might have a fit halfway up a tree or hanging upside down by his knees on a climbing frame. The hospital had made him a crash helmet and he was very pleased with it, so that if he fell his head would not be damaged. But Danny never fell.

His parents had discovered Danny's condition was not so rare; that at least one person in every two hundred has some form of epilepsy and most of these people lead perfectly ordinary lives. They found there was an Epilepsy Association they could join which gave them all the information they needed. And after a while they got used to Danny's epilepsy.

By the time he was old enough to start school he had almost stopped having fits, but his parents went to see the headmistress and told her all about Danny.

Miss North had taught children with epilepsy before, so she was not too worried. She promised to treat him like an ordinary boy because, as his mother said, quoting the consultant, that was what he was.

'Except,' she said, blushing a little, 'that we think he's rather bright.'

Miss North had also taught children before whose mothers thought they were rather bright, so that did not worry her either.

Danny was not the only child in his class with a problem. There was a boy with asthma who had to bring an inhaler to school, another with eczema which gave him far more trouble than Danny had ever had from epilepsy. And a little girl on a special diet who had to wear a label on her dress warning people not to give her the wrong things to eat.

The school doctor came to the class to talk to them about these conditions and he told the children, in a very simple way, why they must never give Tania sweets or crisps and what to do if Danny had a fit.

His one attack, on the football pitch, attracted far less attention than the game itself. Danny had been in school nearly four years before he had a fit in the classroom.

3

By that time he was in Miss Pringle's class.

Danny's hospital doctor was delighted with his progress and after his last check-up decided to reduce his medication.

'One attack in three years,' he said, pleased. 'I think we can risk it.'

And of course there was always a risk, any time medicine was altered. But Danny was not too worried.

'If I have a fit, I have a fit,' he said to his mother who on the whole preferred him not to. 'And if I have one at school – don't worry. Miss Pringle can deal with anything. You should have seen the way she dealt with Mr Maguire.'

Danny chuckled at the memory.

'Go on, then. Tell me,' said his mother.

'Mr Maguire came roaring into the school to complain that his darling little daughter had been brutally attacked by her teacher, because Miss Pringle had tapped her on the wrist or something. And he's 6 ft 3 and you should have seen how angry he was.'

'Well he should have gone to the headmistress if he had a complaint. What did Miss Pringle do?' Danny's mother was fascinated. She had no idea school life was so dramatic.

'Oh she just did the helpless lady bit,' said Danny. '*You* know...' He made a simpering face, widening his eyes and lowering his eyelashes in such a wicked imitation that his parents laughed. 'And Mr Maguire ended up APOLOGISING... and saying he'd give his darling daughter a belting for being such a nuisance to her lovely teacher.'

Mrs Blane was very impressed and agreed Miss Pringle did indeed sound very capable.

Danny put his teacher to the test just two days later. It was during a sum test that he began to feel very strange. It was a feeling he could never describe but he knew what it meant. When he stood up Miss Pringle looked at him with a frown, for during a test she suspected any interruption, but her expression changed when she saw Danny's face.

He was very pale and looked troubled. He went to Miss Pringle and said as though he sounded a bit sick: 'I'm going to have a fit.'

And he meant, immediately.

This is it, Miss Pringle told herself, trying urgently to remember all the advice she had been given by the school doctor and finding her mind blank. One thing she did know. No matter how nervous she might feel, she would hide it well. Hoping there would be time to take Danny to the medical room she asked him if he hadn't better lie down. Danny did – on the floor, which had not been what she had in mind.

The class stared, some with the joyful look which

welcomed any diversion; one or two with eyes filled with alarm.

'Danny,' announced Miss Pringle, hearing with relief that her voice sounded perfectly normal, 'is going to have a fit.' She managed to make it sound everyday, as though he had been asked to read aloud or work out a sum on the blackboard. And on cue, Danny's body stiffened.

As his muscles contracted, he cried out and several children jumped for it sounded as though he was afraid or in pain.

'Don't you remember,' Miss Pringle said calmly, taking off her jacket which she was planning to put under Danny's head. 'The doctor explained that would happen. Who can remember why?'

She was grateful for Stephen Craig who never could resist showing he knew the answer to a question and always did know.

'Air being pushed through the voice box, miss,' he answered promptly.

'Very good, Stephen,' said Miss Pringle.

Danny was rigid.

'He's dead, miss,' cried Tracy in a voice trembling on the brink of panic.

'Nonsense, Tracy,' said Miss Pringle and welcomed the automatic snigger which ran round the class when anyone was snubbed. But she knelt beside Danny and unobtrusively felt his pulse. He was still for less than a minute and suddenly began to jerk.

'Thought you said he was dead, Tracy,' muttered the girl next to her.

Miss Pringle quickly slipped her soft folded jacket under Danny's head. His arms, his legs, his whole body shook convulsively and his head banged harmlessly on the makeshift pillow.

The children were on their feet now, but interested – not panicking. Miss Pringle could see there was no point in expecting them to ignore such an event, particularly during a sum test, so she decided to treat it like a lesson.

'Now we are finally seeing a fit,' she said, straightening up and walking casually away from Danny. 'Can anyone remember what this kind of attack is called?'

34

And of course Stephen knew. He waved his hand.
'Grand mal, miss.'

'Right,' she said. 'And we are going to let Danny get
on with it.' She glanced at her wrist watch and saw that
three minutes had passed since the beginning of the fit.
Only if it lasted more than five, would she need to
summon help.

'Miss, he's choking, miss,' cried Tracy.

'He is NOT choking, Tracy,' said Miss Pringle
firmly. 'It sounds as if he is choking, but he is not.' The
children were reassured. If Miss Pringle said he wasn't
choking, he wasn't.

It seemed to the teacher that Danny's spasms were
less severe now. With a lightening of the heart, she
realised the fit was coming to an end, but he had just
one more shock for her. As the jerking ceased, Danny
became very limp. There was no sign of breathing.

Resisting the impulse to rush to his side, Miss Pringle walked casually over to him and suddenly remembered, with relief, that she had been warned to expect this too. She saw a faint tinge of blue round Danny's mouth, for he had been deprived of oxygen during the attack, but already this was fading. She turned him gently on his side and relaxed as she saw his breathing return to normal.

Hiding her relief as she had her anxiety, she said to the class: 'There now. That wasn't too alarming, was it?'

'No, Miss Pringle,' chorused the class, still staring in fascination.

'Then why are you not getting on with your work?'

Miss Pringle was Scottish, and her voice, when she was becoming impatient rose at the end of a sentence as if in amazement. Heads bent quickly over sum test papers.

As Danny slowly woke up, Miss Pringle asked him quietly if he would like to go to the medical room. Some people, she knew, need to sleep after an attack, but Danny was one of the lucky ones who recover quickly. He was a bit confused, but he looked round at the class, working quietly. And most of all he wanted to be back at his desk. His tongue was a little swollen and he knew he must have bitten it, but apart from that and a slight headache, he did not feel too bad.

One or two of the children stared at him curiously, but most gave him encouraging smiles from behind their test papers. No one was embarrassed or frightened and Danny felt grateful. He thought how awful it would be to go to a school where people panicked just because someone had a fit.

There were dozens of questions at break.

'What did it feel like, Danny?'

'Was it like a bad dream?'

'What could you see? You looked as if you could see something really scary?'

'Did it hurt?'

Danny could tell them very little. He knew nothing at all about the fit itself. But he had a question to ask. He had never seen a fit, and recently he had wondered – what did it look like?

There was no shortage of volunteers anxious to show him and he stared, unbelieving, finally beginning

to laugh as the children vied with each other to imitate the fit, arguing and contradicting.

The best answer to his question came from Gary, a boy who regarded himself as really cool, claimed to have conned his way into 'A' films and knew the pop charts off by heart. 'You looked,' he told Danny, 'like a disco dancer who has gone over the top.'

They all thought that was hilarious and the roar of laughter brought the playground duty teacher rushing round the back of the school shed to find out what they were up to.

The children told their parents about it that evening and most of them reacted perfectly normally, interested to hear all about it, glad that Miss Pringle was so cool in an emergency.

But one mother behaved very strangely. She stalked into Miss North's office next day, to tell the headmistress she thought it 'disgusting' that a child like that should be in a class with what she called 'normal' children.

Miss North concealed her indignation and looked politely puzzled.

'Why?' she asked.

'Surely I don't have to explain why,' said the parent. Miss North waited in interested silence, and her visitor said impatiently:

'It was a terrifying experience for a child.'

'Oh Danny wasn't in the least terrified,' Miss North said reassuringly. 'He understands a great deal about his condition and he's very sensible.'

The parent did not waste time saying it had not been Danny she was worried about, but she could see the interview was not going as she had expected. She was determined to state her case.

'That boy might have a fit at any time,' she persisted.

Miss North felt the time had come to be firm.

'Any one of us might,' she said, and managed not to smile at the look of outrage on the woman's face.

'Oh, it's true. I didn't know either until Danny started plying me with leaflets. He considers me very badly educated, I'm afraid. Anyone can have a fit. Just think how often we say "I nearly had a fit".' And

privately she thought, I'll bet you nearly had a fit when Ronald told you about Danny. She saw the woman's face become a little pink and knew she'd been right.

'Well, yes. But we don't mean it literally.'

Miss North always found it a help on such occasions to become very school-mistressy. She said now, in a teaching voice: 'We do. There is a point beyond which anyone would have a fit. People with epilepsy reach it more rapidly. They can raise their tolerance level with medicine and Danny's dosage had just been reduced. Once it's adjusted again, his epilepsy will be back under control. He may never have another fit in his life.'

She could see the parent was looking less sure now and she reflected more kindly that she knew what was really troubling her. Her son Ronald was quite a clever child, if not such a genius as his mother believed. She worried constantly about anything which might, as she put it, hold him back.

Miss North said, gently: 'Danny's a perfectly ordinary little boy, you know.' She smiled and added mischievously: 'Except – we think he's rather bright.' She wished Mrs Blane could have heard that.

'You mean he's NOT backward?'

'Now, where did you get that idea?' asked Miss North.

'Well, I thought he must be. Being epileptic.'

Miss North sighed and wondered sadly how many people had the same idea, but she spoke patiently.

'Having epilepsy doesn't make a child backward. You know, I don't usually discuss individual children, but would it comfort you to know that Danny has about the highest IQ in that class?'

And that was naughty of her, because she knew it wouldn't comfort Ronald's mother one bit. But it did end her complaints about Danny.

Danny's medicine was adjusted again and, in spite of the hopes of one or two of his classmates, there were no more attacks.

Gradually everyone forgot about his epilepsy. And that is why, unfortunately, no one thought to mention it to Mr Masterson.

4

Mr Masterson was the new games master, in charge of all sport and gym, and his coming to the school changed Danny's life.

At first it was marvellous. The new teacher was very athletic and very keen. He was also very tough and everything had to be done his way, but the children thought he was terrific.

There was no larking about in Mr Masterson's gym. He brought out all sorts of apparatus the last master had never bothered with and told them to treat it with respect.

'It's a privilege, not a right, to use this equipment,' was Mr Masterson's most repeated phrase. 'And never forget it. You have to earn the right.'

The gym class suddenly became the most exciting event in the school week and even children who had always thought they were no good at it, blossomed. Danny had always enjoyed gym and to be given access to so much equipment was just like Christmas. He just seemed to know the right way to climb ropes, to balance on the beam, to use the rings.

Mr Masterson spotted quickly that Danny was

talented and encouraged him. Wayne was good too and a girl named Sharon. One or two of the others were a bit inclined to show off and Mr Masterson had no time for daring. Safety was his main concern in the gym, and after one or two sergeant major blisterings, they got the message.

Danny was very happy. He loved everything about the gym, even the smell – a mixture of old plimsolls, leather and rope. He began to spend most of his free time there, helping Mr Masterson, who did his own maintenance because he didn't trust anyone else.

Mr Masterson started having special coaching sessions for those who wanted to try for the gym award, B.A.G.A. and he kept a close watch on Danny and Sharon. Sharon had a true ability and grace and she brought what she learned in a ballet class to her free

style routines. Mr Masterson began to dream of entering them both for the schools championship and that was something he would never do unless he thought they had a chance of winning.

He was quite annoyed when Danny told him he would have to miss a coaching session one day. He had to go to hospital for his routine check-up.

'What's wrong with you?' asked the teacher. 'Athlete's foot?'

'Epilepsy,' said Danny.

The teacher's reaction puzzled him, for he seemed horrified. Danny decided he was teasing him. Mr Masterson was a great joker.

The gym teacher was not joking. As soon as Danny left he stormed off in search of the headmistress and found her in the sunniest spot in the playground where concrete had been dug up to make a garden. She was supervising the top class who were making a rockery, but when she saw the fury on the teacher's face, she told the children to work on by themselves. She drew him away from the group so they could talk quietly.

His anger was all the worse because he had to keep his voice down.

'Why,' he demanded, 'was I not told that boy is an epileptic?'

Her first thought was that Danny had had a fit and no one had told Mr Masterson how to cope with it. When she realised he hadn't, she was glad but apologetic. Of course the teacher should have been told Danny had epilepsy.

'But surely,' she said, 'it makes no difference?'

'NO DIFFERENCE,' he roared and the gardening group looked up with quick interest, scenting a drama. The teachers hastily walked farther away, Mr Masterson muttering all the time.

'No difference . . . that lad spends half his time hanging upside down in my gym . . . MY GYM . . . my responsibility . . .' He went on like that for some time and Miss North waited until he had run out of words.

She explained that Danny rarely had attacks; that he had ample warning if he was going to have one. And when she could see that reason was getting her nowhere, she asked, rather coldly: 'What exactly frightens you, Mr Masterson?'

He made an obvious effort to speak more calmly.

'There was a boy at my last school. Epileptic. He used to drop. Like a stone. Imagine that happening to a lad balancing 6 feet up on a beam.'

'And was that child allowed to use dangerous equipment?'

'Of course not.'

'Quite right. If Danny's epilepsy was like that I expect his parents would have asked to have him excused.'

They walked up and down the playground, Mr Masterson's voice occasionally rising, attracting interested attention from bored pupils in neighbouring classrooms. Miss North's arguments were having little effect.

'He's an epileptic,' the teacher repeated stubbornly. 'And as far as I'm concerned, that's all I need to know. I'll allow no risks in MY gym.'

'He's not,' said Miss North, hoping to surprise him and succeeding.

'Not what?'

'Not an epileptic. His fits are epileptic. He isn't.'

'So what difference does that make?'

'It's bad English for a start,' she said drily. 'But if you think about it, it's a label. It lumps everyone with epilepsy together as though they were all the same. And that's what you're doing with Danny Blane. You've known one boy with epilepsy and you expect Danny to be just like him.'

'With respect,' he said heavily – and it was a phrase which Miss North knew meant 'with no respect at all' – 'I don't think you know much about epileptics.'

'I've taught enough children with epilepsy to know no two are the same, any more than two children with red hair. And that's what you are implying when you talk about "epileptics".'

Mr Masterson abruptly lost patience with the discussion.

'Look, I'm prepared to call him anything you like. He's a great kid and I don't want to do anything that will hurt him. I'm just not prepared to let him take risks under my supervision. And that goes for apparatus work, swimming. . . .'

'Swimming,' said Miss North, dismayed. 'Oh dear.'

'Anything that would be dangerous should he have a fit,' said the gym teacher firmly and strode off, leaving the headmistress to stare helplessly after him, wondering who was going to tell Danny.

Miss North hurried off to find Miss Pringle and urge her to have a word with Mr Masterson. Not only was she Danny's teacher, she was very persuasive and the gym teacher liked her, as all the staff and one or two of the pupils was interestedly aware.

Miss Pringle caught up with him as he left school, but his welcome turned stony when he realised she only wanted to talk about Danny.

'It will break his heart if you stop him from doing gym,' she said, looking appealingly at Mr Masterson. Danny would have recognised the expression on her face. It was the one she had turned so successfully on the angry Mr Maguire.

'Better than breaking his head,' he answered firmly. 'In any case there's lots of work he can still do in the gym without being a danger to himself.'

Miss Pringle could imagine Danny's reaction to that.

'At least let him swim,' she pleaded finally. 'He's a natural swimmer. He's probably safer in the water than you are.'

It occurred to her afterwards this might not have been the most tactful way to put it.

'He'll be even safer out of it,' said Mr Masterson in a tone which hinted the discussion was closed. They walked in hostile silence until they came to Miss Pringle's bus stop. Then, because he did not want her to think too badly of him, Mr Masterson tried to explain.

'I'll tell you what really bothers me. He's a competitive lad. Keen to go in for badges, galas, championships. Now sure – all right – he's fine where there's no strain, no tension. He's probably safe enough at the pool, messing about with the others. What worries me is – how will he react to stress?'

Now if Miss Pringle had kept her wits about her, she could have answered that. She knew very well how Danny would react. She had been there, cheering him on, when he won the cup at the Sports. But, angry at Mr Masterson's obstinacy, hurt at her failure to change his mind, that incident had gone right out of her head. She remembered it afterwards but felt, sadly, it would probably make no difference if she did tell him about Danny's victory. And there she was wrong. It would have made a lot of difference.

She stood silently at her bus stop, her disapproval written on her face, taking a somewhat exaggerated interest in passing vehicles. He made a last attempt to justify his decison.

'There's a lot of pressure on a boy going in for championships. I wouldn't take a chance on an epileptic ...' he corrected himself ... 'a young lad with epilepsy under tension. Show me how he behaves in a crisis. And if I'm wrong I'll be the first to admit it.'

5

Miss Pringle tried to prepare Danny for the shock, but he could not think what she was talking about. Gym work to be restricted to vaulting and mat routines? No more swimming? She HAD to be joking.

When he realised this was serious, Danny's amazement turned to horror. Since tears were out of the question, he took refuge in rage. He knew it wasn't Miss Pringle's fault, but at that moment he felt he hated her for bringing him such news. Her tone was kind and sympathetic but he heard only the words.

'I suppose YOU told him,' he said furiously. 'About that fit I had in the classroom.'

'Danny,' she said reproachfully. She had taken him into the cloakroom so they could talk privately and he shrank back from her against a row of pegs, his white face framed by duffels and blazers.

'It's never been a secret,' she said gently. 'You've always been open about epilepsy and that's why no one has ever worried about it.'

'Then why is HE worried?' muttered Danny. He couldn't bring himself to mention the teacher's name and he was not yet prepared to believe the worst of Mr Masterson.

'He doesn't understand,' said Miss Pringle. It was difficult for one teacher to discuss another with a child, even if they disagreed in private.

'Then I'll explain,' said Danny eagerly. 'I'll tell him about epilepsy . . . that I hardly ever have attacks. And I have a warning.'

Miss Pringle looked at him. 'It won't make any difference if you do, Danny,' she said. 'He doesn't think he's being unkind or unfair, he thinks he's being careful.'

Danny knew then that Mr Masterson had already been told, and still did not understand.

He asked if he could go and see Mr Masterson right away, but Miss Pringle kindly pointed out that he

would be in the middle of a gym lesson . . . and that *they* should be doing geography. There were curious looks when they went back to the classroom and Danny suddenly felt miserable. Everyone would know soon and he couldn't bear it. Maybe he could talk to Mr Masterson at break; make him change his mind.

He saw the track-suited figure twice at break, but each time failed to catch his attention. Once Mr Masterson seemed locked in talk with another teacher and absently walked away as Danny approached. The second time he suddenly interested himself in an idle game of football and sprinted off in another direction. It occurred to Danny the teacher was avoiding him. It was a whole new thought to him that an adult could behave like that.

Somehow the news spread, although Danny told no one. Sharon heard it even before the next gym lesson and she was horrified. She rushed off to look for him and found him moodily kicking a pebble around on his own.

'Danny, it's awful. It's unfair. He can't D O that . . .' she began but Danny cut her short.

'Why should Y O U care?' he said rudely. Danny had never been so rude and unkind to anyone before, but he did not want to talk about this to Sharon. He felt she was gloating because he was the only other one in the class as good as she was, and that was mean of him. Sharon was near to tears but he didn't notice. He was so hurt himself he didn't care how anyone else felt. Sharon kept away from him after that.

Before a week was out quite a few people kept away from Danny.

He dreaded the next gym period. Would he be told
in front of everyone that he must not use the apparatus?
When the boys went into the locker room, Danny
impulsively made up his mind not to change into gym
kit. They all gathered round him excitedly when they
realised, asking questions. No one had ever cut gym
before. Danny stood up and fiercely told them to shut
up and leave him alone. Then they trooped out, almost
all turning back to look and not in a friendly way since
he'd been so threatening. And suddenly he was alone.

Danny felt a bleak triumph. He had surely forced the
gym teacher to come out and speak to him. He would
be angry of course, but at least it would be private. But
he did not. And that was worse.

Before the bell rang for the end of the lesson, he crept into the corridor and found himself face to face with Miss North.

'And what, may I ask, are Y O U doing here?' she began severely. 'Where S H O U L D you be, young man?'

'Gym,' muttered Danny and the headmistress gave him a look of sympathy which he did not see for he was avoiding her eyes.

'I see,' she said and hesitated. 'Would you like to come and talk to me about that? After all, you've nowhere better to go, have you?'

'What's the use,' said Danny and she raised her eyebrows. Then he brightened. 'Couldn't you talk to Mr Masterson instead? He'd listen to you.'

'I have, Danny.'

He suddenly lost his temper and his head.

'I thought a teacher H A D to do what the head told him,' he cried, too upset to consider the wisdom of such scorn. 'Or do you mean you're on his side?'

Miss North had never allowed a child to speak to her like that before. But she could not remember a child having to cope with such bitter disappointment before either.

'Be patient, Danny,' she said and tried to sound encouraging for she still hoped to change the teacher's mind but she did not want to raise Danny's hopes too high.

He gave her a look of despair.

'Can I go, now?' he asked with flat politeness not too removed from insolence.

'You may,' she said.

Danny began to dream of revenge. He would join the Sports Centre gym club and win the championship for THEM. Then Mr Masterson would be sorry. He could see him now, at the finals, his own pathetic team coming nowhere and Danny Blane scoring top. But the Sports Centre cost 30p a session. Danny could not afford many of those. Nor did he have enough money to train at the local pool for the All Comers Gala.

The one thing he was determined not to do, was tell his parents and he had quite a few reasons for that. He dreaded his father, a man with a temper, coming up to the school and making a fuss like Mr Maguire. HIS daughter had been jeered at for days afterwards. Danny didn't really think his father would, but he did not want to risk it.

Also his conscience was bad. Since he'd been told the news he had been sulky and unco-operative, and he suspected that Miss Pringle was thoroughly tired of him. He did not want his parents to hear that.

But his real reason for not telling them was that he knew how pleased they were that epilepsy had made no difference at all to his life. He simply could not bear to disillusion them.

Danny had to change his tactics for the next gym lesson, for Mr Masterson came into the changing room before the session and under his stern eye, Danny sullenly put on his kit. But if he could do no interesting work, he would do none. He spent most of that lesson standing in a corner with his arms folded, looking bored.

Mr Masterson kept his temper. He knew how

Danny felt and he knew he had handled it badly by leaving others to tell the boy about his decision. But he was still convinced he was right. Instead of cuffing him and telling him not to be a fool, which was his inclination, he suggested Danny might like to use a mat.

'Thank you, sir,' said Danny and to everyone's surprise ran off to the locker room. He reappeared carrying a comic, sat cross-legged on a mat and began to read it.

'O U T,' roared Mr Masterson. And Danny left, sauntering, making faces at the other children on the way out so they would laugh. Danny had never had an enemy before, but he felt he had one now and he was determined to behave as badly as he dared.

One day he was really insolent. Mr Masterson had asked Danny to help set up the beam – a responsible job usually regarded as a compliment by the children asked to do it. But Danny felt he was being taunted. Why should he set it up when he wasn't allowed to use it any more. To refuse would not only mean punishment, it would look as though he minded too much.

Instead he said eagerly, 'Me, sir? Oh thank you, sir. Do you think I can manage, sir? I'll be ever so careful, sir.'

The class richly appreciated such a jest, until they saw the anger on the teacher's face and wisely fell silent. Danny waited for wrath to descend, but Mr Masterson controlled his annoyance and said, quite mildly: 'Don't strain yourself, lad. I'm sure someone else could do the job without all the drama.' And he nodded to Wayne who jumped immediately to his feet and ran smartly to the beam.

'Creep,' said Danny savagely to Wayne at break.

'Well, what did you expect me to do? Tell him to put up his own beam?'

And Wayne walked off leaving Danny, as he so often was these days, alone in the playground.

There was one thing worse than gym. At least there Danny had the satisfaction of taking on his enemy in battle, but the swimming sessions were pure misery.

He hadn't believed at first that he wasn't going to be allowed to swim any more. Everyone knew he was a good swimmer. There was a silver cup in Miss North's office to prove it.

The first time he watched the class go off in the coach to the pool without him, he stood in the playground and felt his eyes ache with tears he refused to shed. And then he believed it.

He had been told to regard it as a free period – a chance to do his homework. He should really have been put in with another class for there was no teacher free to supervise him, but Miss Pringle told him she was sure he could be trusted (and hoped she was right. The old Danny could be trusted. She was not entirely sure about the new one).

Danny sat miserably in the classroom, trying to think of some way to force Mr Masterson to change his mind, when suddenly he thought of something he could do.

Creeping out to the playground, he edged alongside Miss North's office and listened outside the window. He was sure the room was empty. Danny tiptoed in and looked around quickly. It took him some time to spot the cup he had won at the Sports, because although it had been given a place of honour at the time, so had lots of other things since. It was lost behind the football shield, the dancing trophies, certificates and endless offerings made by the children to Miss North.

'Typical,' he muttered bitterly to himself. 'Shows how much they care.'

He seized the cup, shoved it under his blazer and hurried back to the classroom. He looked through all the desks until he found a plastic carrier bag, wrapped up the cup and hid it in the cloakroom. He was not entirely sure what his plan was. He half thought he might show it himself to Mr Masterson.

What would be much better, he reckoned, would be for them to realise the cup was missing and make a fuss. Mr Masterson would be bound to hear about that, then Danny could come forward and give it back.

By the end of the day he had elaborated that day-dream until he'd reached the point where the gym teacher insisted on placing the cup in the trophy cupboard in the gym. He even might apologise, thought Danny adding the finishing touch to his fantasy, publicly.

When he realised no one was going to notice the cup was missing, Danny took it home and handed it to his mother.

'Oh,' she said, pleased. 'They're letting us have it for a bit, are they. Now I call that very nice.' And she put it on the mantelpiece.

'Well it's mine, isn't it. I won it,' said Danny listlessly.

'Of course you won it,' said his mother. 'But it belongs to the school. See.' She handed it to him, pointing to the engraving. 'It has been presented to the school and your name is the first ever to be put on it. Maybe if you win it three times they'll let you keep it. Mind you, I doubt it. It looks a valuable thing to me. Here ...' she laughed. 'I hope no one steals it while we're responsible for it.'

Someone already has, thought Danny, his heart sinking. Not his. And valuable. He was a thief now.

His mother either did not notice his gloom or decided to ignore it. The Blanes had become all too accustomed to Danny's moods lately and they were worried.

If Danny had worn a sandwich board stating 'I am totally fed up' he could not have advertised his gloom more obviously. He took to walking with his

shoulders hunched, chin on chest, eyes down. His legs seemed to have become wooden and he stalked about as though looking for something to kick.

In spite of this he really believed he was suffering in silence; keeping his problem to himself. He was surprised when his mother first asked him what was wrong.

'What do you mean?' he asked guardedly.

She meant why didn't he come crashing home from school full of news and complicated exciting plans, eat a huge tea, rush off to play with the boys who lived round about and come in, only under protest at the latest possible hour saying he was starving.

All Mrs Blane said was: 'Aren't you feeling well?'

'I'm feeling fine,' muttered Danny.

'You don't act fine,' she commented. But she could see that Danny was not going to tell her what was bothering him and she let it drop until his father came home from work.

'What's wrong with *you*?' asked Mr Blane, eyeing his dejected son. Danny shrugged.

'He SAYS,' Mrs Blane answered for him, glad of an ally, 'that NOTHING'S wrong.'

Danny scowled and saw his parents exchange a look.

'Maybe he'll talk to *you*,' Mrs Blane said to her husband later. 'I know something's worrying him.'

'He'll get over it,' Mr Blane said easily at the beginning. He felt his wife worried too much about Danny. 'Most likely he's fallen out with Wayne or something. Or maybe his teacher's given him a telling-off.'

After a gloomy fortnight even Mr Blane was worried about Danny.

Mrs Blane had tried ignoring her son's mood. She tried being extra cheery herself. She even became impatient.

One weekend she made another attempt to find out what had happened to change Danny so much. Instead of running in, full of joy because it was Friday, Danny had trudged home and immediately turned on the television set. He sat glumly in front of it watching a programme designed for pre-school age children.

'There's a programme in Hindi on the other channel,' his mother suggested ironically. 'It would make as much sense to you as that.'

Danny gave no sign that he'd heard. Exasperated, his mother put herself between Danny and the set and stood looking at him, hands on hips.

'Look, love. If something's worrying you, tell me. Maybe I can help.'

Danny sank farther back into his chair. 'Nothing's

worrying me,' he said with a weary patience that made his loving mother feel like giving him a good smack.

'Then in that case, I think it's about time you stopped giving us a hard time and cheered up a bit,' she said briskly. 'Now – why don't you go out to the square and play football?'

'Do I HAVE to?' he asked with infuriating politeness.

His mother felt her temper rise. She moved quickly and with a violent twist of her wrist, switched the set off.

To her surprise, Danny just went on sitting in his chair, staring at the empty screen. Neither of them spoke until Mr Blane came home and a meaningful look from his wife accompanied by a toss of her head in the direction of her son, told him all.

Danny looked up, suddenly aware of the gaze of two concerned faces and felt angry. Why couldn't they leave him alone? If they knew what he was keeping from them just so they wouldn't worry, they would be grateful.

It did dimly occur to him that he wasn't handling his secret sorrow too well, but he wished they wouldn't just stand there; looking at him.

'Is it all right if I go to bed?' he asked, saying the first thing that came into his head.

'At seven o'clock?' His mother was incredulous. 'What on earth is wrong with you, Danny Blane?'

'What's wrong with me is everyone asking me what's wrong,' shouted Danny. 'Can't I even go to bed now without a lot of questions?'

He jumped with alarm when his father suddenly bellowed at him.

'You certainly can go to bed and that's the best place
for you if you can't keep a civil tongue in your head.
But first you'll say sorry to your mother.'

'Maybe it's just his age,' his mother said, when
Danny was out of earshot.

'Whatever it is, it's gone far enough,' said Mr Blane.
'And I'm going to find out what it is, even if I have to
go to that school and ask.'

'Don't do that,' his wife said, hurriedly. 'If anyone
goes, it had better be me. You should hear him talk
about fathers who turn up at school. Besides you'd
have to take time off work.'

'As long as one of us goes. It just isn't like our Danny
– all that slumping in front of the telly, face so long it's
tripping him. And where are all his mates these days?'

That night before he went to bed, Mr Blane
suddenly announced:

'I'm thinking of taking Danny to the game
tomorrow. They're playing at home.'

Mrs Blane, who knew her husband had not been
planning to spend his Saturday at a football match and
would normally have reminded him the vegetable
patch needed attention, was delighted.

'He'll like that,' she said.

Danny did. He began to look like his old self as he wound his scarf round his neck and searched his room for his woolly cap.

They walked to the ground, Danny jumping up to swipe overhanging tree branches along the way and going on to his father about their team's chances. He even waved when he saw Wayne and his brother going into the terraces and made a cheeky face as he headed with his father towards the stand entrance. Actually Danny preferred the terraces. It was not only £1 cheaper, he liked the atmosphere and he always got a good view. But there was no denying it was very impressive to go to a match with your father. Wayne, after a second's surprise at seeing Danny grin again, grinned back and pushed his nose up with his finger – sign language for 'posh'.

Every time Danny went to a match the magic worked. The roars, the smells, the colours and the excitement always made him feel good. At half-time Mr Blane casually asked if he would like a hot dog and Danny said fervently: 'You bet.' When Danny raised the money to go to a match by himself there was none left over for hot dogs.

I'll tell him, he suddenly thought and the decision made him feel good. After the match, I'll tell him. Maybe he'll even know what to do.

As the player Danny most admired wove between murderous opponents to shoot what surely had to be the winning goal, he turned in a frenzy to his father.

Mr Blane was shouting encouragement, rising to an exultant yell and Danny knew he felt just as he did. He'd been crazy not to tell his father. But the yell died to mingle with a groan from hundreds of throats. Danny's hero had missed. Minutes later the other team skilfully passed the ball down the field and scored. The whistle blew. It was over.

As he turned to leave the ground, it seemed to Danny that everyone had turned up their coat collars, as if shutting out the defeat they had just witnessed. He glanced at the row behind him. After a win there was a hysterical feeling that every stranger was a friend.

Now the crowd shuffled out, each man alone in his disappointment. Danny glanced militantly round to see if he could spot anyone wearing the other team's colours, so he could hate them. And his eyes met those of Mr Masterson, cheerful and victorious.

On the way home Danny hardly spoke.

That very evening Mrs Blane wrote a letter to Danny's headmistress. A few hours in the company of not one but two depressed football supporters had finally pushed her to the point of feeling she could no longer bear the atmosphere of her own home.

What, she asked herself, would she do if the school couldn't help. She could tell from homework books that his teachers were also having trouble with Danny. Scribbled comments on his work grew more and more impatient as she turned the pages.

The sight of the silver cup – as she glanced round the room for inspiration – encouraged her. Mrs Blane was cheered to remember how cooperative the school had always been in dealing with Danny.

She decided to ask Miss North if she could come to see her. By coincidence, the headmistress had also decided that a talk with Danny's parents was essential and she had written to the Blanes, wisely trusting her letter to the post.

The date she suggested was a swimming day. Mrs Blane went off to keep her appointment believing there was no danger of bumping into Danny who knew nothing about it. She had seen him take his towel and trunks that morning. But Danny always did, in case his mother noticed. He might well have seen her cross the playground if he'd been sitting in his classroom where he should have been. But he wasn't.

Danny had decided to play truant.

6

He wanted to do something really wicked and then if
he was punished at least he would know why and he
decided on truant for several reasons. He was just plain
bored, sitting all alone in school. And it would be a
challenge to see if he could escape without being
noticed. It was bound to be exciting, he felt, wandering
free during school hours. And truant had the attraction
of being a major offence in everyone's eyes.

His classmates would be amazed that he had the
nerve to do such a thing. And if he was caught, he
reflected bitterly, it would show the school what he
thought of it.

Misery was having a very bad effect on Danny. He
felt he hated them all – even teachers he hardly knew.
Mr Masterson was a popular member of the staff and
whenever Danny saw him off duty he was always part
of a joking, friendly group. Even his own Miss Pringle
obviously liked him. Danny felt, quite unreasonably,
that if she was really on his side she would have
nothing to do with Mr Masterson.

This was really amazingly conceited of him. To
most of the staff the ban on Danny was just one inci-

dent amongst the dozens which make up a school day. Whether they sympathised, because one or two also had prejudices about epilepsy, or were opposed to the decision, they had quite simply forgotten it. And that is what Danny found so hard to forgive.

Everyone but him seemed to have accepted the situation. Danny Blane did not do swimming or gym. And that was that. He had expected a bit more solidarity from his friends. They could have come out on strike or something. But they hadn't even given him a wave when the coach left that day. It did not occur to him this might have something to do with his bad temper lately.

Well it would serve them all right, he thought, if they came back and found him missing. In fact he had no intention of being caught out. He planned to return to school long before the coach did.

He would like to have strolled boldly across the playground and out of the main gate, but he didn't quite dare. And that was just as well. If he had, he would have met his mother, hurrying to keep her appointment with the headmistress, planning what she would say.

As she took a seat in Miss North's office, Danny was climbing the wall behind the infant block. He dropped into the street, which somehow looked quite different in forbidden time.

'There's something I ought to have told you, Mrs Blane,' Miss North began and was sorry to see the look of alarm her words inspired.

'Danny's not in trouble, is he?' asked his mother anxiously.

Danny was. He knew the minute his feet touched the ground he was not going to enjoy this as much as he thought. He had a strong desire to get back into the school again. His plan had been to go to the market, wander about the stalls and buy an apple. But suddenly he felt very conspicuous. He had left his blazer, which he could have used on this chilly autumn day, on a peg, but even without that to identify him, he was obviously school age. What if someone reported him? What if he met someone he knew. He began to feel a bit like a criminal on the run and it was not such an enjoyable experience as he had imagined it would be.

Miss North was making a cup of tea to put Danny's mother at her ease.

'He's having a bad time,' she said, adding with a smile, 'and making sure everyone around him does, too. But it's not his fault and I'm very glad of the chance to talk to you about it.'

When she had told Danny's mother there was a long silence. Mrs Blane did not trust herself to speak and knew she must control herself before she said anything. She was so sad for Danny she could almost have wept but she was also very very angry.

To gain time while she brought her feelings under command, she said stiffly: 'It's kind of you to be so sympathetic, Miss North. I can see now why you let him bring the cup home.'

She could tell immediately the headmistress had no idea what she was talking about. Her eyes went to the

place the cup should occupy, then to Mrs Blane.

'Oh dear,' said Danny's mother faintly.

At about that very moment Danny had seen a policeman at the end of the street and made up his mind. He must go where there would be few people about and that meant the banks of the canal.

That, he knew, was really wrong. The canal was forbidden not only by the school but by parents and Danny knew perfectly well why. The bed of the water was a thick tangle of weeds and creepers and children had drowned in that canal.

He shrugged. He wasn't planning to swim in it after all, just walk along the towpath. Besides, to someone who has stolen a silver cup and ducked out of school, what was one more crime.

He wished he hadn't remembered the cup, which was worrying him a great deal. He could have returned it easily and probably no one would ever notice it had gone. But what would he tell his mother?

In her office Miss North suddenly saw the funny side and laughed. 'So he just picked it up and took it home? Now, I wonder how he is planning to get himself out of that predicament.'

And Danny's naughtiness over the cup rather cooled Mrs Blane's hot indignation over the way he had been treated by Mr Masterson.

In a rather easier atmosphere the two women continued their discussion of Danny's future and decided not to send for him to join them until they had talked it out thoroughly.

And that gave Danny time ...

His guilty, self-absorbed walk along the forbidden
path was interrupted by the appearance of another
child, this one far too young to be a fellow truant. He
was a small blond boy, wearing striped dungarees a
little too big for him and earnestly carrying a plastic
bucket.

Danny looked round for the adult who was sure to
be in charge of such a small boy. To the sort of law-
breaker he had become, all adults were a threat. He
was puzzled to see no one, then noticed a slightly open

garden gate leading to the tow path. The child had greeted him with the incurious friendliness of people under three, and Danny wondered uneasily if he should take him home.

Tripping slightly over the legs of his dungarees, the little boy stumbled purposefully towards the thick, brown water.

'Hey,' called Danny, in alarm.

'Seaside,' the little boy explained, and hurried on, dangerously near the edge. Danny wondered afterwards if he could have stopped him, but it happened so quickly, no one could. He had begun running even as the little boy tripped again and this time seemed to somersault into the canal. He did not even bob up to the surface.

Danny had dived in after him within seconds but it seemed to him a frighteningly long time before he even found the child, lying still under the water.

He grabbed the boy's arm but had to shoot to the surface himself, his head almost bursting. He dived again and this time he rationed his air supply quite professionally, his life-saving lessons coming back to him. But pulling a living, healthy boy from a swimming pool had not prepared him for saving an unconscious child.

The weight of a two-year-old amazed him even as he struggled to the surface and for a moment all he could do was tread water, supporting the boy so that his face was clear.

He struggled with his burden to the edge of the canal then, obeying an instinct, he turned the child upside down, holding him by the ankles and staggering a little to keep his balance. He was comforted by the sight of water pouring out of the boy's mouth.

'Cry,' muttered Danny. 'Please, cry.'

The child, his face colourless, was silent.

Danny placed him face down on the tow path and knelt over him, pumping his back. When he had all but despaired, tears rolling unnoticed down his cheeks, he turned the limp little body round, pinched the nose closed and began to breathe into his mouth.

He actually felt the tiny lungs begin to work and the artificial gasps give way to regular breathing. He saw the pale blue eyelids flicker and the frightening tinge of purple which had begun to colour the small face, give way to pink. And Danny let out a war cry of pure joy.

This fearsome noise completed the recovery process. The child opened his mouth and bellowed. Danny grinned. An adult might have scooped the boy up and comforted him, but Danny sat back on his heels and beamed with satisfaction like a music lover at a good concert.

The child's mother heard the noise and ran on to the towpath, looking frantic. The boy's howls, the mother's screams at the sight of her drenched child roused the neighbourhood. It struck Danny how very silent the whole episode had been until then. When he remembered it later it was always like a slow motion film seen through very thick glass.

Suddenly the towpath was full of people and in a very short time, drowning the excited voices congratulating, questioning and thanking Danny, came the siren of an ambulance.

'Oh no,' said Danny, remembering where he should have been.

He tried to protest, but every adult on the towpath seemed determined to get him to hospital, with the little boy he had saved, for a check-up. Shivering under an adult jacket which someone had thrown round his shoulders, Danny had no choice.

Fifteen minutes after the ambulance had rushed away from the canal the telephone rang in Miss North's office.

She excused herself to Mrs Blane and answered it, her official manner changing to alarm. Mrs Blane tried not to be curious, but she wondered what bad news the headmistress had heard.

Miss North was looking at her with anxiety and something very like pity. She hung up and said:

'Mrs Blane I don't know what to say. Danny seems to have had some sort of accident. He is in hospital.'

7

Danny's mother assumed at first that he had only had a fit.

'People WILL call an ambulance,' she said, fairly calmly. 'They mean well, but it's not necessary. Oh well, I'd better go and bail him out.'

Miss North shook her head. 'No it's not that. The person who rang me said Danny had been in the canal and his clothes are drenched. She said to bring dry clothes.'

The two women stared at each other, sharing alarm and puzzlement.

'I'll drive you home to get his things,' said Miss North. 'And we'll go to the hospital together.'

Danny was waiting for them, redly shining after a hospital bath inflicted on him by a mortifying orderly who was under the impression that all boys were incapable of scrubbing themselves. He was wearing strange pyjamas, the top too small and the trousers too long, under an institutional dressing gown with a numbered tape sewn on the lapel.

'Here he is,' the casualty department sister said, leading Mrs Blane and Miss North to Danny. 'Here's our hero.' She stood back, beaming, clasped hands resting on her large apron. Danny grinned sheepishly, not at all certain what reception to expect after his truancy.

His mother hugged him thankfully and over her shoulder, Danny met the cynical but amused gaze of his headmistress.

'What a fright you gave us, young man. I think an explanation is in order, don't you?'

Fortunately for Danny, there was a diversion.

He had been put in a side ward off the casualty department and the door of the room burst open. In rushed the little boy Danny had saved and he had obviously had the same treatment as his rescuer. His newly washed blond hair stuck up in spikes and he was wearing the same eccentric night gear as Danny. He was followed by his mother, more composed now than she had been when they shared the ambulance journey, and smiling.

'Oh don't be angry with him,' she said charmingly to Miss North. 'You can't imagine how brave he has been.' She took her little boy's hand. 'There, Robin. Say "thank you" to Danny.'

Robin shook his head and Danny blushed with embarrassment.

The child's mother frowned. 'Robin, Danny pulled you out of that horrible canal. If it hadn't been for him, you would have drowned.'

But Robin didn't know what drowned meant. And although he could remember falling in, he couldn't remember being pulled out.

'Don't you WANT to say thank you?'

Robin considered. 'No,' he said positively, and everyone laughed. Robin laughed too, pleased that he had made a joke.

'No what,' said his mother quickly, knowing what his response would be.

'Thank you,' said Robin, promptly and looked pleased again at the mirth he seemed to have provoked.

'And I'd like to thank you properly, too,' said

Robin's mother and planted a kiss on Danny's scarlet forehead. Mrs Blane could see it was time to rescue her son from his admirers.

'I'm proud of you,' she told him, as Miss North drove them home.

'The whole school will be proud of him,' said Miss North. 'How are you going to like being a hero, Danny?'

He thought about it. 'It's going to be a bit embarrassing,' he said.

'It might have its compensations,' said Miss North with a smile.

And it did. Teachers who had come to regard him as a thorough nuisance greeted him with clasps on the shoulder and beaming smiles. School friends who had been put off by his surly phase, crowded eagerly round him in the playground.

Danny could not keep a smile from his face. There was just one disappointment. The teacher he most wanted to impress, Mr Masterson, was not there. Mr Masterson had broken his leg doing what he told his pupils never to do – running along the edge of the swimming pool.

He heard the news though. Miss Pringle visited him specially to tell him.

'Now you know how Danny behaves in a crisis,' she could not resist saying. And he nodded, full of remorse.

'Tell the lad . . .' he began, but she interrupted him, smiling.

'You tell him,' she suggested. 'It will be worth a lot more, coming from you.'

And she left a copy of the local newspaper on his bedside table. There was a picture of Danny on the front page.

The newspaper had sent a reporter and a photographer to interview him the day after the accident and they insisted on taking pictures of him on the towpath. They wanted the little boy, Robin, in the picture, too, but his mother, shuddering, refused to let him go near the canal.

Danny was asked a lot of questions, but fortunately not the one he dreaded – 'what were you doing on the towpath during school hours?'

'Is it true you're an epileptic?' asked the reporter.

'It's true I have epilepsy,' he answered carefully and tried to explain, but he could tell the reporter wasn't paying attention.

'How did you feel when you saw the kid go under? Were you scared? Have you had life-saving lessons? Did you have to give the kiss of life?'

90

The newspaper came out three days later and the headline on Danny's story read: 'EPILEPTIC SAVES DROWNING BABY.'

Danny took the newspaper into Miss North's office and found her desk already piled with copies.

'I told them it was wrong to say I'm an epileptic,' he said.

Miss North gave him a very meaningful look.

'You can't win them all,' she said. 'At least they didn't say "TRUANT saves Drowning Baby".'

Danny looked at her guiltily and to his relief, saw laughter in her eyes. He knew, gratefully, that was all she was going to say about that.

Even when the excitement died down, it wasn't over, for Danny had been recommended for a Royal Humane Society award and a few weeks later he was told he was to receive one.

Two policemen came to the school to present it and at the sight of them Danny remembered his feelings of guilt about the silver cup – now restored to its place of honour in Miss North's room. There was a full assembly to see the award and a lot of visitors. Mr and Mrs Blane sat in the front row with the school governors and the parents of the boy Danny had saved.

The reporter was there, too, and this time Miss North spoke to him so Danny knew they'd get it right in next week's newspaper. He had great faith in Miss North.

The ceremony ended with a speech from the child's father who also had an award for Danny – a cheque for £100. £100! Danny had often thought what he and his

friends could do with that amount of money. It was one of their favourite games. He could certainly afford to join the Sports Centre now.

It was at that moment he noticed amongst the audience, a crutch leaning against his chair, Mr Masterson.

At the party provided in Danny's honour after the ceremony, the gym teacher hobbled up to him and they looked at each other in silence for a moment, Danny embarrassed and wary. A quiet had fallen in the hall and everyone heard Mr Masterson's opening words.

Perhaps Mr Masterson intended everyone to hear, for he was a generous man, well able to admit when he had been wrong. And what he had to say was in the nature of an apology.

'It's a good job everyone didn't take my attitude, lad,' he said clearly. 'It's a good job SOMEONE taught you to swim.'

There were quite a few people who felt like cheering when they heard that, but instead a tactful buzz of conversation broke out and everyone looked away, leaving Danny and the teacher to get on with what they had to say.

'Sorry I was rude, sir,' said Danny awkwardly and the master grinned.

'Rude?' he repeated. 'You were unbearable. But that's enough of the fancy talk. We've a lot of lost time to make up. Don't think this crutch means I can't supervise.'

'You mean the B.A.G.A., sir?' said Danny eagerly.

'And the all-comers. And the championship. Or have you had enough awards?'

'Not yet,' said Danny grinning. 'Next time I get one, it will be gold.'